BALTO

THE MOVIE STORYBOOK

Adapted by Jane B Mason

Based on the motion picture story by Cliff Ruby & Elana Lesser

Screenplay by Cliff Ruby & Elana Lesser and Roger Schulman & David Cohen

Hippo
HOLLYWOOD

UNIVERSAL PICTURES AND AMBLIN ENTERTAINMENT PRESENT "BALTO" VOICE TALENTS OF KEVIN BACON BRIDGET FONDA PHIL COLLINS BOB HOSKINS MUSIC BY JAMES HORNER "REACH FOR THE LIGHT" BY BARRY MANN JAMES HORNER CYNTHIA WEIL PERFORMED BY STEVE WINWOOD STORY BY CLIFF RUBY & ELANA LESSER SCREENPLAY BY CLIFF RUBY & ELANA LESSER AND DAVID STEVEN COHEN & ROGER S.H. SCHULMAN EXECUTIVE PRODUCERS STEVEN SPIELBERG KATHLEEN KENNEDY BONNE RADFORD PRODUCED BY STEVE HICKNER DIRECTED BY SIMON WELLS AMBLIMATION G GENERAL AUDIENCES All Ages Admitted DTS STEREO IN SELECTED THEATERS DIGITAL dts SOUND IN SELECTED THEATERS MCA SOUNDTRACKS A UNIVERSAL PICTURE UNIVERSAL AN MCA COMPANY

© 1995 UNIVERSAL CITY STUDIOS, INC. & AMBLIN ENTERTAINMENT, INC.

PRINTED IN U.S.A

10/2/95

NSS# 950209

Scholastic Children's Books,
Commonwealth House, 1-19 New Oxford Street,
London, WC1A 1NU, UK
a division of Scholastic Ltd
London ~ New York ~ Toronto ~ Sydney ~ Auckland

First published in the US by Grosset & Dunlap Inc., a member of The Putnam & Grosset Group, New York, 1995
GROSSET & DUNLAP is a trademark of Grosset & Dunlap Inc.

First published in the UK by Scholastic Ltd, 1996

ISBN 0 590 13954 1

Made and printed in Italy

10 9 8 7 6 5 4 3 2 1

It was a crisp autumn day in New York City's Central Park. As colourful leaves whipped around their feet, a grandmother and granddaughter walked their little husky puppy down a shady path.

"It was here somewhere," said the grandmother.

"What are we looking for, anyway?" asked the girl, kneeling down to pet her puppy.

"A reminder of a wonderful story," the grandmother said, smiling. "It happened in a small town in Alaska, almost on top of the world..."

During the cold winter of 1925, it snowed hard in Nome, Alaska. Back then, the fastest way of getting around was with teams of dogs pulling long sleds. Races were held every year to find the fastest dogs...

"It's the three-mile marker," Balto barked to his friend Boris. "We don't want to miss the finish. Let's cut through town."

The Russian snow goose rolled his eyes. But before Boris could protest, Balto took off. He scampered over rooftops, trotted across drainpipes, and leapt over puddles, while Boris struggled to keep up.

A happy little girl named Rosy and her pet husky, Jenna, were heading towards the finish line, too. Balto stopped long enough to watch them pass. "Jenna," Balto sighed. He'd never seen a dog half as pretty – or half as nice. Balto wondered if he'd ever get to meet her face to face.

Then suddenly, all eyes turned back to the race course. At last, the first sled was rounding the corner. It was led by Steele, the fastest – and meanest! – dog in town.

"Come on!" Rosy cheered. She took off her furry musher's cap and waved it in the air. Suddenly a gust of wind blew it out of her hand. "My hat!" Rosy cried. Steele and his team were heading straight for it at top speed!

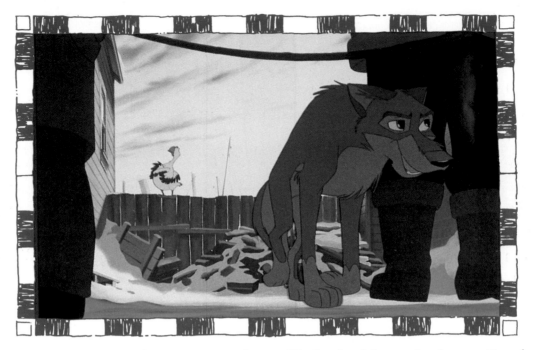

Across the street, Balto sat up in alarm. He looked from the hat to Steele and back again. Then, like lightning, he dashed into the street.

"It's that wild dog!" cried a spectator. "He's trying to ruin the race!"

Still racing at top speed, Steele bared his teeth at Balto. "Out of my way, wolf!" he snarled.

But Balto paid him no attention. He ran alongside Steele for a second, then darted in front of him and snatched up the hat with his teeth. Steele and his team roared past, missing Balto by barely a hair.

Steele's team crossed the finish line and the crowd cheered – everyone, that is, but Rosy and Jenna. They were gathered around Balto.

"Balto, what a crazy thing to do!" Rosy exclaimed as she took the hat from him. "And just to show off to Jenna."

Jenna and Balto smiled at each other shyly, and Rosy gave Balto a hug.

Then Rosy's dad stepped forward. He had a broom in his hand. "Rosy, stay away from that dog!" he warned. "He's a half-wolf!"

Balto's proud smile quickly faded. It was always the same story. No one trusted him – just because of a little wolf blood. And so, head down, Balto headed sadly out of town.

By the time Balto and Boris reached their old abandoned fishing-boat home on the outskirts of town, the sun was low – and so were Balto's spirits.

Boris had a feeling his friend had more on his mind than Rosy's father's harsh words – and he was right.

"It's Jenna," Balto finally confessed. "But she's not my type."

"And why not?" Boris asked. "Is it this wolf business again? Is love. So go make move!"

A few days later, Balto got his chance. He spotted Jenna peering through the window of the house that served as the town hospital.

"Jenna?" Balto said, coming up behind her.

"Oh, hi, Balto," Jenna said sadly. "Rosy's in there. She feels hot and she has a bad cough."

Balto climbed up next to Jenna and looked into the hospital room. The doctor was just finishing taking Rosy's temperature.

"It looks like diphtheria – the eighteenth case this week," the doctor said sadly. "And I'm out of medicine."

The doctor was worried! That night, he sent a telegram to Anchorage asking for more medicine. But the news he got back was not good. A huge storm was brewing in Alaska. No planes or boats or trains could get through. There was only one way to get the medicine – dog sled!

The very next day, a big race was held to find the fastest, strongest dogs to pull the sled. Steele and his musher would be the judges.

At last – this was Balto's chance! He knew he was fast and strong, and he had to help Rosy! But Boris wasn't so sure.

"Balto! Are you nuts?" he cried. "They would not put you on the sled team even if you did win!"

"Wish me luck, Boris," was all Balto said.

Seconds later, the starting gun went off. Balto tore down the course. Soon he was at the front of the pack, running neck and neck with the lead dogs.

Sprinting ahead, he inched his way past one dog, then another, and into the lead. Then Balto crossed the finish line – first!

Jenna watched him from the sidelines, and her heart swelled with pride. But Steele was not happy, not one bit.

"Do you honestly think any musher would put you on his team?" he growled jealously. "No way am I running with a wolf dog!"

The other dogs knew better than to argue with Steele. Balto would not be on the team.

By evening, the new team was in place, and the whole town came to see them off.

"Good luck! ... Safe journey!" the townspeople called as the team started off, while on a ledge outside town, Balto sadly watched them go.

Several nights later, the team picked up the medicine and loaded it onto the sled. Then Steele and his team began the long journey home. But the storm was quickly growing worse. Soon the trail was completely covered by snow.

"Steele!" one of the dogs yelled. "Maybe we're lost. Maybe we should turn back!"

But Steele kept struggling against the wind and ice. "I am *not* lost," he growled. "I am not lost!"

But he was.

Back in town, the bad news spread: Steele and his dogs had missed the second checkpoint. They were off the trail!

Meanwhile, Jenna waited in the hospital with Rosy, who was quickly getting sicker.

Watching Jenna and Rosy through the window, Balto knew he had to do something. He had to find Steele and the medicine – fast!

Balto hurried home to tell his friends his plan. Boris, of course, tried to talk him out of it. "You are crazy! You will freeze!" he argued.

But their polar bear friends, Muk and Luk, were ready for an adventure. And when Boris saw he couldn't stop them, he decided to go too.

By that time, Steele and his team were hopelessly lost in the blinding snow.

"We're going in circles, Steele!" the other dogs cried.

But Steele wouldn't listen. "No, we're not!" he shouted back. He never got lost! Steele looked right, then left. "It's ... this way," he said.

But Steele didn't see the sheer slope of ice straight ahead. A second later, dogs, musher and sled were careering down the steep, icy hill!

Luckily, Balto and his friends were already deep into the wilderness in search of Steele. As they went, Balto slashed the tree trunks with his claws to mark their trail.

When they stopped for a rest, Balto sniffed the air. Something wasn't right. "Guys," he said, looking around, "I think we should keep moving."

"Easy to say for a guy with four legs– " Boris started. Then he saw what Balto had smelled. A huge, angry grizzly bear!

Seconds later, a giant claw whizzed through the air. "Yeeaaaaarrr!" Boris yelled.

Balto instantly dashed to his friend's rescue. He dived at the bear, sinking his fangs deep into the grizzly's leg. But the bear was too strong. He threw Balto against a tree, then reared up for the final blow.

Suddenly something raced across the bear's path. Jenna! She leapt onto his back, but she couldn't bring him down. He clawed at her shoulder, and Jenna fell to the ground.

Then the bear turned back to Balto. Fighting, they tumbled down an icy slope, onto the frozen river. *C-R-A-A-A-C-K!* The ice beneath them began to break! In an instant, the bear was swept away and Balto was plunged into the freezing water.

"Geronimo!" Muk cried as he and Luk jumped in after their friend.

"Muk! Luk!" Jenna barked. Then she saw Luk rise up out of the water with Balto in tow. Balto coughed and opened his eyes.

"Balto!" Boris exclaimed. "I was so scared, I got people bumps."

Balto smiled and turned to Jenna. "How did you find us?" he asked.

"I saw your tracks and followed them," Jenna told him, "to tell you that we got another telegram from Anchorage. Eagle Pass is blocked. We have to take the mountain trail." Then she took a small step forward and stumbled. Jenna's shoulder was hurt!

Balto knew that Jenna could not keep travelling. So he made a sled out of a soft tree bough and asked Muk and Luk to pull her back to town. "You'll have to lead them," Balto told Boris.

"You're going on by yourself?" Jenna asked.

"It won't be the first time," Balto replied bravely.

Boris spoke up. "A dog could not make this journey alone," he told Balto. "But maybe a wolf can."

Then Jenna slipped off her red bandanna and put it around Balto's neck for good luck, and they said goodbye.

Balto pressed onwards through the snowstorm until he smelled something familiar. *Steele?!* Balto peered over an icy slope. There was the sled! The dogs were exhausted, the musher was unconscious, but the medicine was fine!

Balto bounded joyfully down the hill, and the dogs looked up. "Balto!" they shouted.

"I can lead you home," he told them. "I marked the trail."

Then Steele stepped up in front of the sled, his eyes narrowed. "*I'll* get us back," he growled. "I'm in charge."

"Then let me at least take the medicine," Balto begged. "The children are getting sicker." He moved towards the sled, but Steele would not back down. He lunged at Balto's throat.

"Look out!" the dogs called. Steele and Balto were headed for a cliff! But Steel did not listen. He lunged once more. A second later he tumbled over the edge.

Balto turned to see the dogs slipping respectfully into their harnesses. He made sure the musher and medicine were loaded securely on the sled, then he took his own position at the front of the pack.

"Mush!" Balto barked, and the team moved forward.

Steele pulled himself over the edge of the ravine just in time to see the sled head out of sight. "Go ahead, wolf dog," he muttered. Then he spied Jenna's bandanna lying in the snow. It had fallen off Balto during their fight. "I'll make sure you *never* get home," he muttered and picked it up.

On his own now and hungry for revenge, Steele moved quickly over the snow. Soon he was ahead of the sled. He came to one of Balto's marks and slashed across it with his claws. Then he made a mark just like Balto's on another tree, and another, and another, and with an evil laugh, he loped off towards Nome.

Soon Balto and the team reached the marked trail. "Which way, Balto?" one of the dogs asked.

Balto looked around. Something wasn't right. The trail went in a circle! "Steele!" Balto gasped. Then he panicked. There was no time to waste. But which way should he go? Balto began to run.

"We're going too fast!" the dogs cried as they tore through a thicket of trees … and straight towards a jagged cliff.

Balto stopped the sled just in time. But the crate of medicine kept on going. Balto leapt out of his harness and onto the cliff's edge and skilfully caught the crate in his teeth.

"Yeah!" The dogs cheered. Then they stopped as the snowy ledge gave way under Balto's feet and down he fell.

By now, Balto's trail had led Steele back into town. He was telling all the dogs that Balto had gone crazy and stolen the medicine.

"He grabbed the crate," Steele lied. "But he couldn't handle the sled. He didn't see the ice, or the cliff..." Steele pulled out Jenna's bandanna and tossed it at her feet. "He made me promise to take care of you," he told her.

Jenna put the bandanna back on. "You're lying!" she told Steele. "Balto's alive, and he's coming home!"

Balto was alive. But how would he ever make it back up the steep cliff to the sled? Then Balto saw something – wolf tracks in the snow! They led right up to the top of the ravine.

Balto picked up the medicine and began to follow the tracks. He looked up ahead and saw a pack of wolves watching him.

"*Aaa-whooo!*" One wolf howled his encouragement. Boris's words echoed in Balto's head – *A dog could not make this journey, but maybe a wolf can* – and, one foot after another, Balto made his way up the steep cliff to where the other dogs were waiting.

"Let's go home!" Balto barked.

Quickly, the sled dogs got into their harnesses, the medicine was loaded, and once again they headed for Nome.

Jenna was sitting by Rosy's bedside when a wolf howl suddenly echoed through the night. *Balto?!* She ran to the window and saw him lead the dog sled into town.

Boris, Muk and Luk were there to see him too. "Not dog. Not wolf," Boris declared. "He is hero!"

While the doctor unloaded the medicine and gave it to the children, Jenna and the whole town gathered to cheer for Balto.

"He has the most endurance ... the most fidelity ... the most intelligence..." one dog exclaimed.

"Yeah!" said another. "They should build a statue of him!"

"Wow, Grandma Rosy!" the little girl said. "Did Balto do all that?"

The old woman nodded. "That's right. And they did build a statue of him. Right here!" She pointed to a statue of a proud sled dog. "The trail that he took is where they run the Iditarod dog sled race today."

The little girl's eyes widened. "Blaze and I are going to practise right now!" she announced, grabbing the dog's leash. "Mush! Mush!"

Grandma Rosy watched the girl run off, then turned, smiling, towards the statue. "Thank you, Balto," she said softly. "I would have been lost without you."